Kiss Me @ Midnight

A Winter Short

OLIVIA SHAW-REEL

'TIS THE

SEASON, Y'ALL...

Wintertime, in my opinion, is so romantic! I am a SUCKER for love stories. This book is not necessarily a *holiday* story, but may all who read feel the joy, spirit, and charm of the season.

To my family and supporters (my *Libby Loves*) who continuously love on me and my books – you have been the GREATEST gifts to me, year after year!

From the bottom of my heart: thank you!

-OSR

KISS ME @ MIDNIGHT

"**M**a'am, I'm sorry, but we're booked to capacity. There's no way to switch around seats or accommodate you and your child, as we are overbooked. Either you take the $300 voucher that was offered or take the seats, as-is. That's the best I can do. *Next!*"

Korrine St. Patrick stared at the airline attendant, who was done up in too much creamy foundation and matte lipstick. She was slightly put off by the hint of irritation in the woman's voice and couldn't believe her ears. One hand gripped a leather duffel bag by its handle, while the other held her toddler's hand with mama bear strength.

"Excuse me? That's 'the best' you can do? You haven't done anything! Did you not hear what I told you? We've had these seats booked for over three months; I picked the seats and you're telling me the day of they've been changed because of an equipment issue? My daughter is THREE! What is she supposed to do on her first flight and I'm not there by her side?"

"Like I said, ma'am, there's nothing more that I can do. My hands are completely tied as we're dealing with a booked-to-capacity flight. Next!"

1

When the woman attempted to motion towards the next customer, Korinne stepped into her line of vision again. Her eyes were narrowed in desperation. "It's...Christmas...Eve. *Please*. I can't hold my daughter, according to your airline rules, but she's allowed to sit by herself with strangers on her first flight, at three years old? How much sense does that make? What are you, a Scrooge?"

The attendant ignored her words. She sighed heavily, and then looked beyond Korrine's head in disinterest. There was not an ounce of compassion or empathy or sincerity to give. "May I HELP the NEXT customer, *PLEASE?*"

Disbelief washed over Korrine's face as she realized there was no point in arguing or reasoning further. Exhaling deeply, she fought back the urge to grab the woman by her neatly braided hair, and tugged on her daughter. "Come on, baby. Let's go before Mommy loses all of her class."

"What's class?" Korrine's daughter, Mylie, wanted to know. Timidly and curiously, she looked up with bright eyes and pouty lips. Her face was identical to her mother's at that age.

"Something that lady doesn't have," Korrine mumbled. "Come on, baby."

The time to board was less than a half hour away, so

she figured she would give Mylie a rundown of what was going on. Hoisting her child up onto her lap, she wrapped her arms around the girl's tiny waist and pressed her lips to her temple. There were hundreds of people walking around them and bustling to terminals with heavy luggage, but for that moment, all she saw was her daughter.

"Baby, listen to me. In just a little while, we are going to get on the plane that will take us to the fun place. Mommy will be a couple seats away from you, which means you have to be a big girl. You have to put on your brave face, okay?"

Mylie nodded, not quite understanding, as she grabbed her mother's cheek with one hand and played with her hair with the other. "Yes, Mommy."

"It's okay to feel nervous or even a little scared but," Korrine reached down to grab Mylie's biggest stuffed animal from her duffel bag, "that's when you hold Mr. Rabbit extra tight and know that Mommy is not far away, okay? It will only be a couple of hours and then we will be at the fun place for a week!"

Mylie nodded again, a wide, toothy grin practically splitting her face in two. "Uh huh. I can't wait for the fun place, Mommy."

"I can't wait either, baby. We're going to have a good time!" Korrine hugged her daughter just a little tighter and tickled the underside of her arms. "We can go to the beach, and eat lots of yummy foods, and spend every day together. Just you and me."

"No Daddy?" Mylie asked unsurely, pausing as she played with her stuffed rabbit's fluffy ears.

Korrine closed her eyes briefly and breathed a sigh of relief. Her eyelashes fluttered, brown eyes meeting duplicate brown eyes. "That's right, baby. No Daddy. Ever. Again. Just you and me, kid."

Mylie smiled widely. "Good. 'Cause I like you, Mommy."

Korrine giggled. Unlike most children, Mylie's first words were Ma-Ma and as hard as she tried to instill the word 'love' in her vocabulary, Mylie always resorted to "I like you." At first it was strange, but now she adored the phrase.

"I like you too, baby. A *whole* lot."

The airline desk attendants called for First Class boarding, followed by Groups A and B. Mylie was Group B but Korrine figured she would situate her child once her group was called. It was one of the smaller planes, but it was booked to capacity, so Korrine knew it would be impossible to switch with someone.

Passenger after passenger brushed past their tucked legs—young, old, black, and white. Some were dressed

4

warmly for the current cool temperatures while others were dressed to reflect the scorching hot temperatures they were heading to. Korrine was comfortable in an oversized, off-the-shoulder sweater, jeans, and ankle boots. Mylie wore a light jacket with her romper, tights, and ankle boots.

Finally, the last groups were summoned to board and Korrine prayed for the best. Her hopes died a little as she realized she was in the exit row. There was no way Mylie would be able to sit with her, even if someone agreed to switch. She eyed the seat for Mylie, 24B, and looked over the half-sleeping guy with a hood over his head, and the nice looking woman near the window who had a pleasant demeanor. This was the perfect scenario. The woman favored a first grade teacher.

"Excuse me?"

Both the woman and man looked her way. "Would it be possible to keep an eye on my daughter? The airline split us up at the last minute and there's no way she can sit with me in the exit row. She's a really good kid, and..."

The woman's blue eyes widened and to Korrine's surprise, she held up a hand. She shook her head of coiled blonde hair, and her small nose wrinkled in distaste. "I don't WATCH children. I barely even tolerate them. She does seem like a sweet girl, and she's super cute, but I'm here on vacation. Sorry."

Korrine lifted a finger in the air and practically shoved it in the woman's face. "First of all, lady. You're sitting in MY original seat. If you were listening to anything I just said, you'd realize that..."

A flight attendant squeezed through, as she twisted the thin red and blue scarf around her neck uneasily. "Ma'am, is there a reason you're holding up the line?"

Only Korrine's eyes shifted to glare at the brunette. "I am trying to get my daughter situated in her seat, since your incompetent airline SWITCHED our seats."

"Ma'am, that's fine, but can you please do so quickly? You're holding up..." The woman sighed, suddenly distracted by someone else, and made her way back in the opposite direction. "Sir, you cannot put that bag there. SIR!"

"Come here, honey." The guy in the seat closest to the aisle motioned for Mylie with his arms. He removed his hood and revealed a dark brown head of neatly twisted dreadlocks that were pulled back with a tie, kind brown eyes that were shielded by black reading glasses, and a five o'clock shadow that heightened his chiseled features.

Korrine looked on as her normally withdrawn child easily let her hand go, and accepted the man's hand. She smiled from ear to ear as he asked, "What's your name?"

"Mylie."

He helped her into her seat, secured the safety belt with a snap, and then winked up at Korrine. "Mylie? That's a pretty name. I'm Cason. Is this your first flight, Mylie?" His voice was animated and made the child beam with joy.

"Uh huh." She nodded, her flowy ponytails bobbing up and down with the movement. "Mommy says we're going to a fun place for Chwismas!"

"A fun place? And where is this fun place? Do you think I could go, too, for Christmas?"

Mylie genuinely looked troubled for a moment. Her shoulders lifted once and then twice, looking from the kind stranger to her mother. "If Mommy pays for a ticket you can come with us. Right, Mommy? Do you have enough money for his ticket too?"

Korrine blushed involuntarily. "Mmm, baby, I don't think the nice man will want to go with us. But we can maybe pick him up a keychain or some other souvenir."

"Would you like a keychain? Or a snot glass?" Mylie asked.

"It's *shot* glass, baby…and—and—why do you know about that?" Korrine blushed again, embarrassed.

Cason's eyes disappeared completely, favoring slits, as

he threw his head back and laughed. Korrine didn't realize her comment was that funny as she returned his laugh and admired the way he licked his lips before speaking, "I'm sure I have enough of those. Tell you what, Miss Mylie. You can just tell me all about your fun trip and that'll hold me over until I can visit myself, okay? That cool?"

"Uh huh! Did you know we're staying at a report?"

"A report?"

"RESORT, Mylie. Resort, remember? That's one of the new big words we learned." Another flight attendant was making her way down towards the trio, so Korrine grabbed her carry-on and nodded towards the row a few feet back. "Thank you so much again, sir...err, Cason. Mylie, behave, baby cakes. I'll check on you in a little bit."

"'Kay, Mommy! See you lata'!"

Korrine's promise to check in went unnoticed as she found herself as almost a distraction to the chatty pair. From the exit row, she could only spot the top of Cason's head, but she could hear their chatter the entire two and a half hour flight to Los Angeles as they giggled and talked about everything from cartoons to preschool to what kind of pizza toppings they liked most.

Korrine couldn't have been more grateful as she sat

back and allowed herself to relax for the first time in a long time. She wasn't normally so comfortable with leaving her child in anyone's hands and especially not with a male stranger, but figured at the least, there were other eyes and ears surrounding them should anything happen.

Even when Korrine scooped up her child an hour into the flight to take a bathroom break, she was quickly shooed away afterward so that Mylie and the man could color in one of her drawing books. Mylie had him completely smitten and wrapped around her tiny finger, and everyone seemed to know it as he softly submitted to whatever the little princess requested. Currently, he was shimmying his shoulders and singing in a high-pitched but beautiful tone to one of the child's favorite songs from preschool.

By the time the plane landed and it was time for passengers to gather their belongings, Mylie was practically begging her mother to let the nice man tag along with them to a local theme park. Cason had instructed Korinne to stay in the exit row as he hoisted the child and his lone bag in his arms and joined her. Most of the passengers had scrambled off and flight attendants were making their final rounds to pick up leftover trash and hand out pamphlets on why they were the best airline.

"Please, please, *please*, Mommy! Can Mr. Cason come

with us?"

Korrine stretched her limbs and followed the pair out into the bustling airport where families rushed to catch flights, security personnel walked with panting canines, independent drivers held up signs for foreign travelers, and couples huddled together in the shadows. Only Christmastime could produce such a scene. Normally, traveling during the holidays was unheard of for her, but it was Korrine's favorite time of the year and especially now that her daughter was able to open and enjoy gifts instead of becoming fascinated with just the gift wrap. She had packed a couple presents for Mylie to open tomorrow and then they would attend the amusement park the following day.

Many people back home told her she would regret taking Mylie to California at such a young age, but her child was different—extremely articulate, observant, and inquisitive, and was already proving to be enjoying herself. Plus, Korrine made a promise to give her daughter the best possible life, one that she didn't have growing up.

"Can he, Mommy?" Mylie's plea broke her from her thoughts.

She looked over to Cason apologetically, who still held onto the child protectively through the sea of moving bodies. Korrine had Mylie's other hand and they walked forward to baggage claim as, well, a family. It was almost weird.

"No, baby, I'm sure Mr. Cason did not come all the way to California to spend all his time with us. I'm sure he has family to visit and important things to do. We can't hold him hostage for the holidays."

"I live here in L.A., actually."

Korrine looked over at the man, widening her eyes in warning. "You're not helping," she gritted through a tight smile.

"Sorry," he fought back a laugh. "I'll, uh, stand over here quietly."

"Do that," she teased.

"But Mommy," Mylie continued, whipping out her famous pouty face—lips that poked out, eyes that widened and became misty, and a chin that quivered to no end. "It's Christmas! You said Santa gives good stuff to good kids."

"Well, he does, baby girl."

"I've been a good girl. Why can't I have Mr. Cason? Don't you want Mr. Cason too, Mommy? Didn't you ask God for a good man the other day?"

Korrine gasped in shock, and then choked suddenly on her gum. Cason also choked through a laugh, as he patted her on the back. Mylie looked back and forth between the two, still not understanding.

"Are you okay?" he asked.

"Fine," she squeaked, tears brimming her eyes, and warmth flushing her face. She could feel the stares of people walking past. She felt more and more uncomfortable and embarrassed the longer she coughed. She couldn't seem to catch her breath and felt faint as she struggled for composure.

"'Scuse me," she managed to whisper, running off from her child and the stranger, which didn't register in her mind until she was exiting the crowded and smelly restroom, and making her way back to baggage claim.

Her heart raced at her irresponsibility, and she vowed to kick herself repeatedly once she had Mylie in her sights again. What was she thinking? Choking or not, she had left her baby with a man—a man she didn't know, and if her eyes were seeing correctly, a man she couldn't find in the moment.

Panic and disbelief set in, followed by blinding anger, as she skimmed the immediate area for her daughter. She grew weak when she didn't see the distinctive ponytails and blur of pink, or the delicate features that matched her own. Korrine raced to baggage claim, pushing past people and calling out Mylie's name, but had no such luck. Finally, just as she approached one of the desks to make an announcement, a laugh rang out that was so heavenly and rich and familiar that made her insides melt.

She turned in the direction of the sweet sound and saw Mylie and Cason walking hand-in-hand, with luggage rolling beside them, and a popcorn bag in her free hand. There were smiles on each of their faces. She breathed a sigh of relief, thanking God that all was well and asking for forgiveness over her moment of stupidity.

"There you are. Feeling better?" Cason didn't wait for her to answer as he continued, "I assumed you would be a while and took her down to get some popcorn. I hope that's okay? Everybody knows airport popcorn is like the best popcorn."

No, she didn't know that. In fact, Korrine wanted to yell at him or slap him, or beat on his chest in frustration. But she did none of those things. It was an innocent mistake on both of their behalf and no one was really to blame for the carelessness of the situation. He didn't realize how terrible he had made her feel in that instant, with walking off with her child unannounced, and she hadn't really thought out clearly how suddenly leaving her daughter with this man was a no-no, despite choking uncontrollably.

Korrine reluctantly returned their smiles and bent down to scoop Mylie up onto a hip. Her hands were shaky as she rubbed Mylie's back, holding her extra close. She reached out to grab their duffel bag from Cason and thanked him with a smile. "It was really, really nice meeting you. I can take it from here, though."

"Yeah, you too. And nice meeting you too, Miss Mylie. Thank you for chatting with me on the plane and reminding me what the season is all about."

Mylie smiled and cleverly gave a thumbs up. "I like you, Mr. Cason."

He chuckled and gave her a high five. "I like you too, kiddo."

Korrine swallowed hard, searching for the words. It was a little alarming and concerning that her daughter had gotten so attached so quickly to a man she had just met. Still, Korrine appreciated her child's compassion and awareness for others. She couldn't help but to place a grateful hand on Cason's arm. "We both thank you for all you've done today."

"My pleasure, truly. If you don't mind me asking, where are you two staying? Would you like me to give you a ride somewhere?"

Korrine studied his face and the sincere expression on it. He looked harmless; everything about him screamed good person, good intentions, and good upbringing. She looked down at Mylie who watched him with adoring eyes, and swallowed hard, weighing her options.

"We um...we should be fine. Thank you for offering though. I'll call a driver."

"It's a madhouse out there and unless you've scheduled someone to come, it'll probably take another hour with the traffic we have. People are traveling and getting off work at this time," Cason explained, checking his watch for added measure. "Trust me, it's no trouble to do it. My car is in the upper level garage. It would make me feel comfortable dropping you two off and knowing you're safe and sound. It's the LEAST I could do."

He was right. Los Angeles was known for their unforgiving traffic and she hadn't a clue as to her first steps in securing transportation. Plus, she would be saving money and getting to their resort much quicker with this option. His actions had been nothing but genuine thus far, and to be completely honest, Korrine trusted him.

Thirty minutes later, they were situated in Cason's luxury car and peering out of the slightly tinted windows as he drove down a back road to avoid traffic. Because there was no car seat, Korrine had placed her daughter on top of her duffel bag and then snugly placed the seatbelt across the child. Mylie sat in the center of the backseat, swinging her legs with Mr. Rabbit in her lap, and pacifying herself with made up songs and aimless, animated chatter.

Korrine was thankful Cason didn't weave through traffic or drive recklessly like the rest of the idiots on the road. He took his time behind the wheel, was attentive, and very mindful of surrounding vehicles.

She had given him the address to their resort and figured he knew exactly where he was going by his simple nod and lack of GPS. They talked comfortably about previous Christmases, their families' traditions, and food they had to eat or else Christmas just wouldn't be the same. The low, almost nonexistent hum of the engine, mixed in with the warmth of the setting sun and Cason's occasional singing soon put Korrine to sleep. She woke up to giggling and shushing.

"Mommy's so pretty!" Mylie gushed, splaying her hands across her mother's face.

"Yes, she is. Shhhh. Let's get the bags while she rests."

"Okay, Mr. Cason!" Weight left Korrine's lap and the pitter-patter of feet was deciphered.

Korrine grinned sleepily, stretching, and then yawning. She straightened her back in the leather seat and watched through the side mirror as Cason leaned into the backseat and retrieved the bag Mylie had been sitting on. He closed the door and then went to the trunk next. Korrine took that as an opportunity to check herself out in the mirror. She was instantly disappointed in her sleep-filled eyes, tangled hair, and indented face. She had been leaning on her knuckles.

"Way to go, Korri. You fall asleep and snore and slob with the first good looking man who looks your way." She shook her head, finger-combing her locks to look somewhat presentable.

"You say something?"

"Mommy's awake!"

Korrine snapped the mirror closed and blushed. "Hey, y'all."

"We didn't want to disturb you. Looks like you needed that rest."

She yawned loudly, unable to stop herself. "I did, thank you. Oh! I'm so sorry. That was not ladylike. Excuse me."

Cason stood back and waited for her to climb out. She didn't miss the way his eyes looked her over appreciatively, slowly. She quickly had to realize the bottom of her sweater had risen during her nap and exposed a sliver of smooth stomach. She was also giving him a good view of her leg and backside that was angled towards him.

"Ready?"

"Yes. But you don't have to do all of this. We can take it from here."

"You're doing it again," he whispered.

"Doing what?"

"Not allowing me to put all my momma's home training to use. Relax. Don't think of this as a burden; I'm just helping out. No biggie, okay?"

She smiled and nodded. What could she possibly say to that?

When they were checked into the beautiful resort, Mylie went on her tangent again on liking Mr. Cason and wanting him to stick around for dinner. Korrine obliged, unable to say no even if she wanted. Much like Mylie, she was enjoying his company. It was nice to talk to another adult for a change.

Both Korrine and Cason were sleepy, and Mylie was on her way, so room service was in order. Korrine ordered food and unpacked bags, as Mylie showed Cason some of the games she'd brought along. Once the chicken tenders and fries were devoured and Mylie was barely hanging onto consciousness, Korrine invited Cason out onto her balcony where they talked comfortably under the stars.

The sky was dark and masked their faces, only inches away from each other and growing even closer as the night marched on. They discussed goals, dreams, past relationships, their faith, their upbringings, and even their favorite flavor of ice cream. Surprisingly, they had a lot more in common than she imagined, and he was happy to have met a woman who wasn't always nose-deep in her phone. She actually had substance and was intriguing and attractive beyond words.

By the time Korrine was standing to her feet and tugging him back inside, the clock read 11:02. Korrine deposited the thick blanket she and Cason had snuggled under and began cleaning up their mess. He lurched forward, helping her by stacking the dishes strategically on the tray and then depositing the tray outside of her door.

He walked back in, shoving his hands in his pockets. "I don't think I've laughed or smiled this much in a while," he admitted. "You and your daughter are so much fun."

"I'm sorry Mylie kind of roped you into our plans for the day. I hope we didn't keep you from something."

"Don't be sorry. I enjoyed myself and wanted to be here. I only wish I could pocket some of her energy for some of my lazy days."

"Right? All that energy. She'll be out for hours, I'm

sure." Both adults smiled tenderly as Mylie seemed to hear her name in her sleep and snuggled closer to her stuffed animal.

"Tired?" He noticed Korrine struggling to suppress a yawn.

"Very. Traveling wears me out every time plus we've stayed up pretty late. I'm usually knocked out by eight. You'd think I would be used to the time changes with my line of work."

"What do you do, if you don't mind me asking?"

She smiled sheepishly. "Performer..." His eyebrow lifted. "...on a cruise ship."

"Seriously?" He grinned mischievously. "A performer, how?"

"Get your mind out of the gutter," she warned playfully, hitting her palm against his chest. "This will be my fifth year actually. I sing and dance at the nightly burlesque shows. I work nine months on and one month off. This is my second week off, so baby girl and I will spend the next week in L.A. before going back to the Baltimore port."

He nodded, impressed. "That's super cool that you get to do what you love and work on a cruise ship of all places. I can imagine you get to see a lot of beautiful people, places, and things."

"We do, but there's never a time to just relax and kick back. As people are vacationing, we're still working and doing a job, so we don't enjoy the ports and stops as much as people think," she explained.

"But you *do* get time off other than the month, right?"

"Oh, yeah, of course. We typically get one day off a week and work one four-hour shift on the weekend. The pay is decent, tips are a lifesaver, and the benefits aren't that great but I love my job."

"Does Mylie travel with you, or...stay home with her father, or...?"

Korrine's breath caught in her throat involuntarily. She tugged on the hem of her shirt that read *Coffee First, Questions Later*. "She um...she's with me on the ship. Her father's out of the picture."

"Oh, I'm sorry." His eyes narrowed as he attempted to read her face.

Korrine cut him off before he had time to question anything, "Yeah, it's just me and her at this time. She'll be starting school next fall, so it may be time for Mommy to get another job."

"She's not in school yet? Wow! She's smart and so mature for her age. How old again?"

"Three. Thank you. She's a great kid."

A comfortable silence took over the room as the adults eyed one another, unmoving. Cason eventually clapped his hands together and then headed for the door, much to Korrine's dismay. She followed behind him and gave him a quick hug.

"Listen. I can't say it enough. Thank you."

"I wish you'd stop thanking me," he said. "I promise, this was my pleasure. Welcome to my city."

"Your city is beautiful."

"*You're* beautiful," he countered, the phrase slipping out easily. His brown skin reddened in a blush, as he realized his slip-up. "God, that was corny."

She also blushed but for different reasons. She couldn't help her next words. "Thanks. You're not so bad on the eyes, either."

They shared secret smiles, exchanged numbers, and then said their goodbyes for a final time. After closing the door behind him, Korrine bounced up and down and did a little dance of excitement. It was flattering to be told by a handsome man that she was beautiful, even in her lounge clothes, and fatigue painted on her face. She walked over to Mylie and took her little girl to their bedroom. Technically there was another bedroom for her, but Korrine knew towards the middle of the night, her daughter would join her anyway.

After bringing the sheets up to her daughter's chin and kissing her forehead, she was startled by a knock at the door. She pulled the bedroom door up and rushed to answer, expecting someone to be at the wrong room. She didn't expect Cason to be standing there, looking sheepish and unsure, but so darn fine. Before she could say anything more, he stepped further in the room, closed the door softly, and then turned to face her.

"I'm sorry in advance."

"What? Why?"

"For this."

He closed the gap between them, his large hands cupping her face and his lips capturing hers. She gasped in his mouth with surprise and then sighed, giving in. His fingertips played with the nape of her neck and the strands of hair that were spilling out of her low ponytail, twirling and brushing them. Their mouths moved in unison, sweetly dancing and sensually smacking. A low moan left someone's mouth; Korrine was sure it was Cason, and Cason was certain it was Korrine. Still, they moved backwards blindly, their bodies close, feet shuffling clumsily, and tongues locking deliciously.

Soon, her back hit the wall and it was evident how they both moaned at the intimacy of their position. Korrine's hand gingerly ran up the length of his muscular torso and chest, enjoying the ripples and muscles. One of his hands cautiously skimmed down the curves of her right side, settling against her hip. The kissing prevailed, slow and sexy, and just what the doctor ordered.

After a few more moments of exploring each other's warm mouth, Cason was the first to pull away as he rested his forehead against hers. Both hands came up and planted on the outside of her head, boxing her in.

"I'm so...so sorry, but I've wanted to do that all day," he breathed, the smell of cologne faint yet intoxicating.

"I'm glad you did," she admitted.

"I'm glad I did too." His eyes opened slowly, his dark lashes unveiling the most beautiful set of eyes she'd ever seen. They were as brown as cocoa, and somehow she knew she could get lost in them forever. "I know we just met, but I don't want this to end. Please call me or something, while you're here. Don't be a stranger."

"I promise I won't," she vowed, touching her swollen lips with her fingertips.

"Merry Christmas, Korrine."

"Is it midnight already?"

He nodded, their foreheads bumping one another again.

"Merry Christmas, Cason," she finally wished back. "Now kiss me again."

THE END

Thank you for reading!

Please consider leaving a review on Amazon/Goodreads, and/or write to the author herself at *info@osrbooks.com***.**

Reviews and word-of-mouth recommendations mean EVERYTHING to the author.

ABOUT THE AUTHOR

Olivia Shaw-Reel has written nearly 30 books before her 30th birthday. Her award-winning novels, *Soul Cry, What God Has Joined Together, and Matters of the Hart: A Tale of the Dysfunctional Hart Sisters*, have become her biggest-selling books to date.

She also hosts *The Reel Love Podcast* with her husband, Paris. Olivia lives in Milwaukee, WI.

Visit the official storefront for updates and to purchase autographed paperbacks at *osrbooks.com*.

Follow her on Instagram, Clubhouse, TikTok, Facebook and Twitter at *@oliviashawreel*.

OTHER TITLES FROM THE AUTHOR

Soul Cry, Vol. 3
What God Has Joined Together, *2-Book Series*
Baptized in Her Seduction: A Church Love Affair,
2-Book Series
Lord, Save Me From Myself, *2-Book Series*
Meet Me at the Altar
Full Court Mess
The Only Gift
Andrue & Sy'mone: An Urban Love Affair, *3-
Book Series*
Can't Leave Him Alone After the Love We Made,
Book 1
Stuck Wit'chu
Sins of a Mafia Princess
Matters of the Hart: A Tale of the Dysfunctional
Hart Sisters, *3-Book Series*
In Love With Everything You Could Be
Stalked by My Pastor, *Book 1*
A Christmas Miracle
Who's Loving You This Christmas?
Saved, Sanctified, & Filled With Anxiety
Compilation

www.ingramcontent.com/pod-product-compliance
Lightning Source LLC
Chambersburg PA
CBHW061506170626
46811CB00004B/1624